HOMECOMING

Thomas K Slee

REFRACTION PUBLISHING

Contents

HOMECOMING

Yet another new planet dominates the cockpit window, and I collapse into my navigator's chair with the best approximation of reverence my cryo-weakened limbs can manage. The chair is cold, and I lean back into it, savouring the chill as it puckers my skin.

My crewmates will tell you that cryo-sickness is like the most luxurious hangover you've ever had and best dealt with by wallowing as long as humanly possible. For Matre Ester and Trill, this means fighting over the closest thing the *Revenant* has to a shower, and for Pac it means nursing that first cold nutrigel for at least an hour. Sometimes two, if Ester's prayers have soothed the shipspirit, and the jump has gone just right.

For me, though, cryo-sickness means privacy. I can put up with the brain fog, the weird twitches and twinges of long dormant muscles coming back to life, even the nausea, the kind that just bubbles away at the back of your throat, because it gives me time. Time to worship with no-one watching, and bask in the silent majesty of the world we are about to explore.

That's how it was the for the first few jumps, anyway. But this is the twenty-second planet we've visited. The twenty-second with the halo of its atmosphere tinged a sickly green-- No. I can't write this one off yet, otherwise what are we doing out here? I have to allow myself time to thaw before I let reality snuff out my last threads of hope.

Because that hope is all we have. It cleanses us of disappointment as we pack up our equipment and put another doomed planet behind us. It gets me through Matre Ester's final blessings before we jump, and it's the last thing I cling to as we slide off into cryo-sleep. The blue mist rises up my chest and I pray that this time, *this time,* I'll wake up, slide into the cockpit and know that we've found it.

A home for our people.

When I dream of that moment, however, I omit the prickling of stasis residue on my skin, the beeps and warbles of the autopilot, the whirr of the life support, and the musk of years gone by. I ignore the signs of sickness we've all come to recognise in the worlds we survey. The traces of the Retribution that sent us fleeing into space. I ignore the knowing, in the pit of my stomach, that once again my hopes will be dashed.

Now that I'm here, in the chair, this next planet gently spinning before my eyes, I pray that I am wrong.

I pray that this planet, that our ancestors once lived on, tended and in all likelihood destroyed, is somehow still whole. Just as Pac would, as Ester would. That's why we're out here, decades and light-years from everything and everyone we know.

But I'm not them. I go further, repeating the mantras handed down by my mother, in secret. I pray that this planet will be more. Not just a home, but *the* home.

Eden. Our point of origin.

Matre Ester's sermons will tell you that Eden is the Lord's home, that we'll all be welcomed there one day, when our time has come. That our ancestors brought forth the Retribution because they strove to reach Eden before their time. But I know that's not true.

I know what my mother taught me. What her mother taught her. That before the Retribution, before the Striving, before there were thousands of worlds there was just one. Eden. Our birthplace. The home to which we will one day return.

I gaze at the silent orb, its swirling clouds streaked with nutrigel yellow and vacsuit grey. I pick out deserts and oceans between the breaks in the clouds, hoping for some clue that might trigger the instincts I've been honing all my life. I imagine that I'm a child once more, nestled in my mother's arms. She's singing and I'm singing with her, a forbidden hymn for our long lost home. While the melody lasts I can pretend that I'm not whispering, alone in the dark, fearful that the others might hear.

I scroll through the log: *Planet 1682B. Local designations: Antevenire; untranslatable.* Antevenire. I roll the pre-Retribution name around on my tongue, dry as the layer of dust that films every surface on this ship. Antevenire.

It sounds old.

My stomach tightens, enough to draw the nausea down for just a moment. *Last records indicate P1682B was a biological resource, terraforming not required.* The clouds break apart, revealing a mountain range capped with snow. I lean forward, all critical thought on hold as foolhardy hope takes over. Snow means water, and water means–

"Ugh."

I jump and my shoulders, still sticky from cryo, unpeel from the seat cover with a wet snap. Under the cover of embarrassment I drop my steepled fingers to my lap, but Pac's not looking at me. He's staring out the window at our destination. P1682B. Antevenire. The straw from a nutri-pack dangles from his lip.

"Lord, it's even worse than the last one." He bangs his fist into the edge of the half open door and it jitters, emits a weary groan. "At least there's only three more to go."

He shakes his head, and redirects his attention to the door, the nutrigel pack now clenched between his teeth. He gives the door another solid whack, something tinkles free, and it slides back home as if it had never been jammed. He nods, casting one more resigned glance at the looming planet. "Maybe I should tag along with you next time, get the disappointment out of the way. Give the thaw an additional touch of gloom."

"Maybe." I say. In my head, *Please don't.*

"Anyway. Shower's free." Pac's pale, stubble lined cheeks are tinged green by Antevenire's sickly reflection. He plucks a fallen fastener from the floor, tosses it up and snatches it from the air. "And Matre Ester wants to get moving."

I take one last look, Antevenire's radioactive pallor clear now that Pac has ripped the hopefulness from my eyes. P1682B. Another dead end. I slip out of the cockpit and head for the shower without another word.

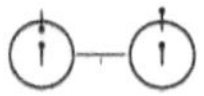

IT DOESN'T TAKE LONG for our first probes to confirm the evidence of our eyes. 1643 local cycles since the Retribution and Antevenire is still roasting from the inside out. We know it's pointless to continue, that the pattern now twenty-one strong will soon become twenty-two, but there's a process. One last probe and a schedule to keep. So we bury our disappointment in our work.

The final probe hangs from the launch bay gantry, and Matre Ester is hunched beneath it reciting her purifications. In private moments, Trill and I joke that she should have been an engineer, not a priestess, such is the precision with which she arranges her sacraments and relics, the fastidious care with which she protects her vestments from the merest hint of grease.

By Ester's side, Trill fusses over the tuning of her low-atmosphere spectrometer; the finesse required for the task balanced by the chaos that follows her wherever she goes. Tools, loose connectors, odds and ends, all resting wherever they might fall. Neither speak, despite the closeness of their work.

I double-check our progress. We're approaching the perigee of our last swing around Antevenire. The launch bay has no windows, but in my mind's eye we're close enough to count every dark valley that separates the bright white peaks. It makes me smile, even though I know now those peaks aren't covered in snow. They're drowning in ash.

Trill sits back, a mischievous glint in her eye, her focus on Ester prone beneath the probe. "Which side of the war was Antevenire on, Matre?"

Pac meets my eye. We both cringe and look away.

"What in Eden is Antevenire?" Ester is buried in the probe's dull silver underbelly, and yet her pinched voice reverberates around the room.

"P1682B." Trill knows she's tempting fate. Her scraggly hair juts in all directions and she leans over, making sure Ester can hear. "The planet we're about to slingshot around and leave behind forever."

Ester pulls away from the probe and fixes Trill with an obsessive's glare. Her head bobs with emphasis. "Are you trying to *provoke* me, Trill?"

Yes. We all know it.

"What side were they on? What *side*?" She holds out an impatient hand. "Tell me, Brother Pac, how many sides were there?"

"Just one, Matre." Pac bows, passing her a mangled fastener and ducking back out of range.

"That's right. The wrong side, and our forebears suffered the Lord's Retribution for their hubris." She keeps her gaze locked on Trill as she pulls her calefactor from within her robes, drops the broken fragment in and clutches it tight in her fist. I groan inwardly, recognising that look. I glare at Trill, but it's too late. "For our arrogance, for daring to pierce the veil between our universe and Eden–

"Time check?" Trill barges between the unbalanced strands of Ester's tirade. Sweat plasters my thin hair to my forehead, even though the life support is set to just the wrong side of freezing.

The countdown flashes its three minute warning. The blip that is us, so close to the planet that we're almost touching, creeps along its glowing path. I buff an old scratch from the corner of the screen. It was scavenged from a derelict older than half the ships in the fleet, so you know it's reliable.

Ester puffs her cheeks. "Blast." She eyeballs the probe with a grimace, knowing it will have to do, and drops to her knees, the glowing calefactor in her lap. "Oh Lord, hear me. Accept this probe, and give it thy blessing."

"LAUNCH BAY READY." The shipspirit intones, almost immediately, and the probe begins to rise of its own accord.

"Not yet!" Ester squeaks. The probe is lifting and she rises with it, her eyes closed, lips intoning the rites of cleansing. In her left hand, her calefactor burns bright orange as it forges a brand new Ring of Eden, the last critical piece. An offering to the Lord, forged from the detritus of our sinful work. The shipspirit ignores her and she's on tiptoes, making the utmost of her stature, working by divine inspiration alone.

"Two minutes."

Ester flings the ring through the open hatch and slams it closed, just as the probe is drawn away. Her shoulders and neck uncurl but Trill refuses to engage, suddenly focused on the probe, its launch commands, its measurement sequence. Her every move is a warning to Matre Ester: Don't. Science is my domain. Not yours.

I hold my breath. Ester's back straightens as she expands, her cheeks as red as the still glowing calefactor in her open hand. I turn away, back to my screen and to my tracking. I don't have to imagine the sermon to come. We've all been in Trill's shoes.

The count spirals downwards, and, in a moment of empathy, a moment of defiance, I give it a shove. I pray that the shipspirit won't mind. Surely thirty seconds doesn't matter. We already know Antevenire is dead.

"One minute."

I time it perfectly, just as the probe is locked into the launch-rack, just as Ester inhales. Lights flash, alarms blare, the atmoshield fuzzes the air, the airlock door splits open and the heat of her rage is sucked into the vastness of space.

The shipspirit takes over the countdown. Thirty. Twenty. Ten. Ester grunts her way through the launch ritual, calling down the Lord's favour, that this last probe might fly true. Antevenire fills the entirety of our vision, raging storms frozen in a picture of grace. Does Ester realise she is praying to the Lord that wrought destruction on this world? I will ever understand her, and I hope she'll never understand me.

A dull thunk reaches our feet. Locks release, thrusters fire. The probe is gone, with the Lord's blessings or without, arcing down and away.

"And not a moment too soon." Pac says, backing away from the atmoshield until he's leaning against the launch bay door-frame, ever-present nutrigel in hand. His grease-covered over-alls feel incongruous against the lifelessness of this metal cavern. When we set off, tt was crammed with probes, instruments and the hope of our entire fleet. Now it feels as empty as I do. "Come on, lighten up, hey? Twenty-two down, three to go. Isn't that worth celebrating?"

Trill snorts, shaking her head. I know what she's thinking. With a nasty glare, she steps over the tools she's left scattered across the grating, knowing our fastidious priestess can't bear the sight of such mess. She pushes past Pac and out of sight without a word.

He takes a long, noisy pull of his gel, but I can't bring myself to look him in the eye. The launch bay doors whirr, and Antevenire disappears from view. We'll never see it again. Our arc, the arc I calibrated both weeks and decades ago, will soon fling us from its gravity well, out of this system, and onto the next disappoint-ment. I know Pac is just trying to bring us back together, but the thought of the four of us eyeing one another around rickety aluminium kitchen table makes my stomach churn.

Ester watches the doors until they slide shut and the atmoshield buzz falls away to nothing. Only then does she acknowledge Pac's presence.

"What would we toast, Brother Pac? Here's to another dead end? To the wrong-headedness of our mission? To the eventual death of every ship in the fleet? One by one, until the Lord's Retribution is complete?"

Yellow-tinged gel dribbles over Pac's tightly clenched fingers. He unfurls himself to his full height, his scrambled hair, brown and tinged with grey, almost brushing against the ceiling. "How about being one jump closer to home? One jump closer to meeting my grandkids before they die of old age?"

His voice cracks, then breaks completely. He turns away to mask the hurt, leaving a trail of gel on the floor behind him. I know how he feels; we all do. We've all left someone behind, knowing that by the time we return they'll be long gone. It's the price we all paid for our hope.

Ester stands as if rooted to the metal floor, her calefactor dangling from her open hand. In a strange way it's a comfort to see her like this. The certainty of her faith stripped away to reveal the person beneath, struggling like the rest of us. I know it won't last long. I want to enjoy it while it does.

I slide from my chair at the launch console, and start tidying the tools and parts Trill has left behind. "We'll find what we're searching for, I'm sure of it." I'm not, but it feels good to say.

Ester sniffs, wiping the damp from the edges of her nostrils with manicured fingernails. She joins me on the floor, sliding Trill's tools back into their slots one by one. I try to do the same, but there are somehow both too many gadgets, and too many places they might live.

"We're not searching for the same thing, though, are we."

Her question startles me. I look up, see that she's staring at me. Those deep green eyes, so open, so pleading. My tongue is stuck to the roof of my mouth. I look away, concentrate on the strangely shaped tools of Trill's trade, while I try to formulate a response.

"We're both looking for a miracle." It's all I can manage.

Ester shakes her head, a smile tugging at the corners of her lips. She's back on her haunches now, Trill's tools forgotten. "We're more alike than you think. Trill is an egotist, Pac's an idealist, or at least he was. But us? We're here because we believe in something."

"But not the same thing." I say, my skin prickling. It just happens. My mother's dream, my purpose: finding the place where it all began, so we can stop running and start living. Until now it was just ours. Just mine. Suspected maybe, but not known. Until I opened my mouth.

I can't put it back.

She reaches out, her fingers hovering halfway between us. It's unlike her to make such a gesture, and I'm certain she read the horror written plain across my face. Still, I can't meet her halfway. Not yet.

"No." She says, softly, looking down, letting her hand fall. "And yes. You believe that the ecclesiarchy is wrong. Well so do I. At least you believe in your craven Eden, somehow spared from the Lord's wrath, with all of your heart." She shakes her head, her long blonde curls swaying gently. "If my learned Brothers had such solidity in their faith, in their certainty of the justness of the

Lord's Retribution, we would not be here at all. But, in three jumps time, I will be right, and they will be dead. So what does it matter, in the end?"

I sit, dumbstruck and inelegant, as Ester's words slowly coalesce into meaning, and some of the pieces fall into place: the ambivalence of our farewell forty six days but also ninety three years ago. The fact that Trill & I were selected at all. To the rest of the fleet, our mission is a desperate last hope, but to Ester, it's a tacit admission that her daily prayers, her rituals and her sacrifices, have been offerings to an empty pantheon.

And that she cannot countenance.

I return to my senses alone in the launch bay, Ester long gone. I tumble the rest of Trill's gear into a box without care, my mind on other things, and I glide through the hours in a daze. The long navigational calculations, the final, pointless confirmation of P1682B's long ago collapse, the silent, reproachful meal where eye contact is avoided by all. They must have happened, but they slip through my memories like post-cryo mist.

Only the jump ritual manages to draw me from my thoughts. Ester delivers a soulful exhortation to the Lord, begging his mercy for our continued reliance on technologies we no longer understand, the very technologies that sparked our downfall and yet keep us alive. Only the shipspirit answers, and Ester receives their words as if they were a bounty from the Lord itself.

Trill rolls her eyes behind Ester's back, an act I once darkly enjoyed, but which now seems mean-spirited and sad. This is Trill's mission. Built from her late nights, buried in the archives, hidden from the ecclesiarchy, identifying each planet that *might* have survived.

But without Ester, without her sacrifices to the shipspirit, to purify the jump drive, cleanse the gravity engine, where would we be? If any one of these systems were to fail, or fall into darkness, we would be dead, the mission lost. Ester may believe the mission a heresy, but I see now that she needs it to fail on its own terms, not hers. We're all believers, in our own way. I hope Trill realises this, one way or another.

Pac, at Ester's side, catches my eye. He has his head bowed, a sonic wrench clutched in his fists, hanging on Matre Ester's every word. The *Revenant* shudders, and he smiles. He knows he's done his part, got this bucket of alloy and thermoplastic running as smoothly as the Lord will allow. What happens next is out of his hands.

The jump ripples through us, raw spacetime dragging and pulling and twisting and plucking, driving us back to the cryo chambers and to rest. The canopy closes over me, the mist rises and the chill creeps slowly, up my legs, up my back.

For the first time, I don't imagine that the next world will be *the* world. Instead, I think of Pac, Ester and Trill, all of us believing with all of our hearts, and I wonder: do I really want any of us to be wrong?

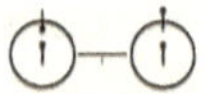

Klaxons.

Calm, dark fog becomes burning light.

Red. White. Red. White.

Blaring warnings, pounding at my ears.

My arms are made of rubber, my fingers paper. I clamp them over my ears and blink, trying to focus. The cryo-bay is spinning.

It's not meant to be spinning. I fumble at my restraints, the only thing stopping me from spinning too.

"PROXIMITY ALERT."

The shipspirit's metallic voice breaks through the cacophony.

"PROXIMITY ALERT."

My clip is halfway undone when the engines roar, and everything that was spinning is now crashing back to an off-kilter reality. My jumpsuit, Ester's hairbrush, Trill's datapad. Tools, chairs, canisters of water. Everything we're meant to lock away before each jump crashes against a wall that is suddenly the floor. But for my restraints, I would have joined them.

"PROXIMITY ALERT."

"Pac?" We need to get to the cockpit. I ooze out of my chamber, muscles the consistency of the cryo-fog, dangling vertical above the floor. Somehow my shaking arms keep me from falling.

I look up. Pac, Ester, Trill, they're all still deep in cryo. Pressed against their canopies by the force of the engines.

"PROXIMITY ALERT."

"I know! What is it?" Shaken, my grip fails and I fall to the wall. I've never spoken to the shipspirit before, let alone yelled at it.

"SCANS INDICATE ARTIFICIAL. ORIGINS UN-KNOWN."

My heart skips a beat. "Did you just answer me?" It skips another. "Did you say *artificial*?"

"AFFIRMATIVE"

This is too much. Far far too much. Why is the shipspirit talking to me? Why did it wake me? Me and not the others? I lean forward, and the long corridor to the cockpit stretches down and down and down beneath my feet. My stomach drops away from my body.

"Lord forgive me." I swallow. Clamp my eyes shut. "Shipspirit, hear my prayer–

The ship lurches, and I know we're done for. My hair stands on end and I hold my breath, waiting for the great outrush of air.

It doesn't come.

Instead, the pressure lifts, my artificial weight dissipates and I realise I'm floating. I open my eyes and it's like a switch has been flicked. Even though I'm upside down, the floor is the floor again, the ceiling the ceiling. I glance up at my crewmates, and a rebellious thought crosses my mind.

"Shipspirit, please wake up Pac."

I watch intently. A light flashes red, then amber then green, and the mist fogging Pac's chamber begins to clear. I don't waste another second, reach out for a handhold, pull myself towards the doorway and careen down the corridor, leaving wet smears of cryo residue in my wake.

For once, I'm not heading for the cockpit. I take a turn, break a seal, and suddenly I'm floating above the gravity engine. A divine complex of glistening crystal, dark and foreboding. It is totally beyond my comprehension, intricate beyond words. All I know is that it's off, and should be on. I don't even know where to start.

"Oh shipspirit, Please, uh, start the gravity engine?"

"UNAUTHORISED. PURIFICATION REQUIRED."

Hmmm. I press forward, away from the safety of the wall. Reach out a tentative hand–

"UNAUTHORISED. PURIFICATION REQUIRED."

I snatch my hand back, and the sharp movement sends me spinning away, out into the corridor where I allow myself to thunk gently into the wall. I glance to my left, back to the cryo bay. Towards Matre Ester, towards the chain of command. And I glance right, to the cockpit, and the 'artificial' obstruction.

Origins unknown.

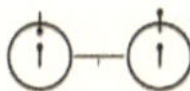

It's not until I'm in Pac's pilots chair that I realise the lights and sirens have fallen silent. I scrabble with the straps, bracing my feet against the console so I don't float away. Only then do I look up. And I freeze.

Beyond the screen, the emptiness is vast. Absolute nothing, just a blackness so deep that the stars feel like glitter on the outside of the glass. No planets, no suns. I've never felt so alone.

My rational brain is trying to tell me this is normal, this is natural. I was born in this same nothing. We all were, my four crewmates and everyone we left behind. The space between the stars has been our home for a millennia. But my racing heart and my clammy hands don't listen. They know that it's a different thing to be lost in the nothing when you're home with the fleet. There are other ships, other people, other sources of food, of fuel, of air. Back home, we're alone in the nothing together.

I breathe in deep, let it seep out slowly through my nostrils. Imagine my mother's hands over mine, slowly relaxing them into the controls' familiar grooves. I regain my center and run through the *Revenant*'s critical systems. The ship responds to my touch: rolling, twisting, beneath and around me, and there is a wet thud from behind.

"Ow!"

"Pac?" I twist around and he comes floating towards the doorway, sweat and slick making his skin glisten in the glow from the controls.

"What in Eden..."

He hangs speechless, eyes wide, entranced. I drop the controls, unclip myself and tug on his overalls, yanking him forward and at the same time dragging myself across to my nav station. His eyes never leave the blackness beyond the screen as he slides into place, his hands falling around the controls as if he'd been flying the *Revenant* all his life.

Under his control, the ship steadies and the stars fall still. I study the curves, the numbers, the charts, trying to figure out just what went wrong. I zoom out to a higher level, covering the entire jump, from Antevenire to P0711M, and I gasp.

"What?"

"Something pulled us out of the jump seven months too early."

But that's not all. There's a new track, flashing magenta to our teal. I zoom in, a twitch of my fingers, and we're falling from a dozen lightyears down to just us, the *Revenant*, listing gently to one side, every line and angle picked out in minute detail. And there, barely ten thousand kilometres ahead, the pulsing magenta path crosses ours. Right where we would have been. A tiny three-legged smudge zips away from us as if we're stationary.

I blink, look again.

"Lord's vengeance." I pull back from the screen, wishing I could seep back into the lining of my seat. "We're not moving."

"No thanks to you." Pac rubs the back of his head, holding the ship steady with just one hand.

"I mean we're not moving. At all." I remember the flashing lights, the blaring klaxons. "The shipspirit must have yanked us out and slammed on the brakes."

"What does that mean?" Pac keeps his eyes straight ahead, peering into the darkness as if we're just on a routine manoeuvre, but I can see the sudden tension in his shoulders, the slight tightening of his grip.

He knows what this means.

I run the numbers in my head. An extra three months in cryo just getting back up to speed. The primary rendezvous gone begging. Years added to our mission.

I don't want to think about it.

I point at my console, flash it up across the screen so both of us can see the artificial object of unknown origin. Speeding away from us, on its path towards nowhere, oblivious to what it has just cost us.

"It means we should check it out. Whatever it is." The years have already been paid. May as well find out what they bought.

"Of all the..." Pac exhales slowly, leans heavily into his chair. Clenches his jaw. "How long?"

"Come on. Bearing 17, mark 3."

"How long, Quae?"

I hesitate. Avoid his gaze. "Nineteen and a half months."

"Nineteen and a half months?" Pac's knuckles turn from blue to white under the console lights, but I don't feel even the slightest tremor from the ship. "For a speck of striving rock? Why would the shipspirit–"

"To save our striving lives!" I cut him off, before he accidentally asks the shipspirit a question. Or worse, gets an answer. A vein pulses on Pac's temple, and the *Revenant* rumbles, as if sensing his anger. The stars shift.

"Bearing 17, Pac. Mark 4. Thrust to zero point two."

"Quae, I'm not–"

"It's not an asteroid." I cut him off. "The shipspirit said 'artificial'. Manufactured."

Pac stares out into space for what seems like an eternity, and I let him. For now, being stationary is a blessing. A second, a minute, an hour is just that. Nothing more.

"You spoke to the shipspirit?" He asks, a hint of curiosity in his voice. "Matre Ester would not approve."

"No she would not." I shake my head, the hint of a smile playing across my lips. "But I asked the shipspirit to wake you. Not Matre Ester."

Pac considers for a long second. He takes a breath. "And it said artificial?"

I nod. He turns away, back to his controls, but I know, in the darkness, that he is smiling too.

Thrust presses us back into our seats, and I rotate the holo as we move. I spout course tweaks, minor adjustments, but my mind is only half here. Already I am out there, building an image of what awaits us, of what called us from our slumber. I tingle with excitement. I know this has happened for a reason.

Pac settles off, and the stars are fixed again. Our green line matches the flashing magenta, and ever so slowly, we're closing in. *One thousand kilometres.* My stomach rumbles. It's been months since I last ate. *Three hundred.* Why are we doing this? We're not salvagers. We have a job to do. *One hundred.* Artificial. Made. By something. Someone. *Fifty.* We're explorers. Hunters. *Ten.* Seekers. *One.*

I flick on the docking lights.

"There!" Pac flings an excited finger at the emptiness. I lean forward. We both do.

There's a bright spark in the distance, and it's growing. Pac pulls back and the ship slides out from beneath us, just a little, as if our uninvited guest is drawing us forward. The spark becomes a dot, then a circle, then a dish.

A final touch of the thrusters and we're locked in together, side by side. It's like we're suspended in medigel, and compared to the stars in the distance, we are. Only the holo shows that we're both flying through space at 61,000 clicks an hour.

It's a strange little thing. A wide, shallow bowl atop an octagonal body, with five arms sticking out from behind: two short and stubby poking from the top and the bottom, two little more than spires trailing behind, and a fifth, long and slender, jutting out at an angle. Trusses, lumps, shines of white, silver, and gold. I can't take my eyes off it.

"It looks old." Pac is on the edge of his seat, leaning left and right to get a better angle.

"Pre-Retribution, definitely." I turn around, imagining Ester's eyes on my back, daring me to voice just how blasphemously old I think it might be. I push her away.

I pull the scan data up on the holo, rotate it left, then right. Cock my head to one side, running the numbers. Yes, it should fit. I focus on the angles, putting Ester's near certain disapproval out of my mind.

"Quae, I think we should wake the others."

I close my eyes, suppress a sigh. Dammit, Pac. Always so... so *faithful*. Can't we keep this to ourselves just a little bit longer?

"You're probably right..." I stall, searching for the right words to stave him off. "But you know what she'll say."

I lean over, trying to let his own imagination fill in the blanks, but Pac refuses to meet my gaze. He's abandoned the controls. His hands are clasped in his lap, spinning the Eden Ring he wears on his right hand, the Ring that the mother of his children had long ago slid onto his finger. The Ring that had once bound them together, before he left them behind for this mission with a promise to, one day, return. A promise threatened by this mysterious hunk of salvage, out in the middle of nowhere.

"We signed up to be explorers, Pac. Not missionaries."

I hold my breath, my heart beating in my chest, and Pac bites his lip. Both of us stare at the dish, the angular, jutting arms and flashes of reflective surfaces. Both of us wondering, I hope, what secrets it might hold.

"Alright." Pac concedes, and my pulse quickens. I'm gripping my console tight. "Let's take a closer look."

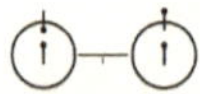

THE RETRIEVAL IS A slow dance. Pac manoeuvres the *Revenant* so that the object, whatever it is, flies below us, directly in line with the launch bay doors while I watch the feed from the corridor outside. I hang there, waiting, Pac's gentle acceleration pushing me back against the wall.

My fingers itch as I double check that the bulkhead is sealed, the atmoshield in place. There's nothing for me to do but stare at the feed of an empty room, the last of our carefully stowed probes tumbling gently in zero-g. Finally, after what seems like an eternity, the launch bay doors open, and I see it through the mess.

A gangly structure of ancient metal, bright against the blackness beyond.

Then, with a light burst of reverse thrust, we swallow it whole.

It makes even less sense amidst the clean functionality of our hanger than it did against the blackness of space. One arm, little more than a stumpy truss, is heavy with oddly shaped boxes and glinting protrusions. The arm opposite is more like a short, stubby tail. The octagonal body that supports the dish is clad with an uneven silvery cloth and is studded here and there with shiny cables, auxiliary structures and, on one face only, a gleaming golden circle. The bowl above reminds me of the dishes some of the oldest cruisers had fitted, wrecks we've never been able to decipher, let alone get working again.

The doors slide shut, closing it off from the vastness outside, and the atmoshield fades away. A thin layer of frost shrouds the object the moment it comes into contact with the air.

It must have been floating out here, forgotten, for thousands of years.

"What are you for? Who built you?" I mutter, sweat prickling all over my body as I imagine Ester's reaction when we finally wake her, show her what we've found. Excitement, unease, trepidation, all that and more boiling over, out of my control.

I kick lightly off the wall, aiming myself loosely at the control panel beside the doorw–

"Aaah!"

My stomach flips, acceleration slamming me to the floor.

Pain shoots down my side.

My head spins.

We must have hit something.

Shit.

"Pac?"

My call echoes down the corridor and I roll to my side. The walls swim before me, and I taste blood on my lips.

There are no lights. No alarms. The walls are walls again. The floor is the floor, the ceiling is the ceiling, and it hits me. The Gravity Engine.

Footsteps behind me. I groan.

Dammit, Pac.

He helps me to my feet. Whispers in my ear. "I'm sorry, Quae. She needed to know."

His big round eyes gaze down at me, begging for forgiveness, and despite the blood seeping from my nose I can't help but smile and say it's okay. Because it is. Whatever it is we've found, it's on board. The decision has been made. Ester can't change it now.

Pac smiles with relief, and we both turn to the monitor. It's so close. The whole thing has settled, resting on its octagonal base. Together we move forward–

"Not one more step!" Ester's shrill voice is amplified by the corridor. "Pac!"

"But Matre..."

"No." Ester marches towards us in just her overalls, cryo-residue slicking her hair across her forehead. I've never seen her so frazzled, she seems incomplete. It's unnerving. "Not until you tell me *exactly* what's going on."

"Pac already told you." Trill's nose is deep in her datapad, and I can see the numbers whirling in her head. "The shipspirit pulled us from the jump–

"Not that." Ester snaps, cutting Trill off, shoving Pac out of the way and slamming a hand against the monitor. She hits it so hard the screen flexes and the image flashes bright green at the edges. "I want to know who authorised *this*?"

She glares directly at Pac, and I see him crumble. "I, uhh…" He can't handle the heat of her admonition. I sigh. He looks so pitiful, cowed before her anger. "I–

"What do you mean, authorised?" I cut in. "It was an emergency. The shipspirit chose us to deal with it, so we dealt with it."

"That has *nothing* to do with–

"We're explorers, Matre, and we found something. Are you really saying we shouldn't even take a look?"

"This is a waste of time." Trill grouches, sneering at the monitor. "It's junk."

"Junk that's been floating out here for *thousands* of years, Trill. Don't you want to know where it came from? Where it might have been going?"

"Right now I care more about where we're *not* going." Trill glares at me, and I'm taken aback. Trill is a woman of science!

"Come on, Trill. You can't tell me you're not a little bit excited. Look at it! What are the mirrors on that long structure for? Those glass lenses, the black tubes? Don't you want to know?"

"I didn't fight for this mission out of curiosity, Quae. I'm here to find our people a new home, so forgive me for not giving a shit about the shiny debris you dragged on board when you should have been recalculating our jump trajectory and getting us back on track!"

My gaze flicks between Trill and Ester, shocked that they're on the same side of an argument for once, that they're both glaring at me, tying my tongue in knots.

Pac comes to my rescue, and when he speaks I sag with relief. "How many planets had you studied six weeks ago? Up close, mind. In the flesh."

Trill's eyes narrow and her lips draw thin. "None."

He turns on me. "And how many system to system jumps had you calculated? Executed?"

"None." I say, wary of where this is going, waiting for him to turn to Ester, bring her back into this when the argument has passed her by. But he doesn't. He stands in front of her, berating the both of us.

"I've watched you and Quae every survey, gushing over this orbit and that cloud layer, your graphs and your measurements, and all the while I've been plugging away in the background, keeping the ship running. Getting us where we needed to go."

He turns to Ester, bowing in contrition, just slightly. "I'm sorry Matre, we should have woken you earlier. But I'm not sorry we brought this machine on board. It might look like a heap of junk to you, but that spindling mess of arms and wires demanded our attention, costing us all two years just to be noticed, and I'll be damned if I don't figure out what it wants to say."

The fraught silence is broken by the shipspirit's toneless interruption, informing us that the scan is complete. No lifesigns, no biological hazards, no traces of radiation. No risk to the crew.

It is safe to enter.

No-one moves.

A bedraggled Ester stands between us and the door. Without her calefactor, her vestments, she seems diminished somehow. Just a regular person, her claims to a higher power stripped away. This must be how Trill has always seen her, I realise, and I smile at the irony. Now, when Trill actually needs her divine authority to hold sway, it is nowhere to be found.

I take a step closer to Pac, stand with him in solidarity. Without me, there is no destination. Without Pac, the ship doesn't even fly. Ester holds on for as long as she can, but Pac isn't even looking at her any more. He's drifted away, to the door, and to our discovery beyond.

Ester throws Trill a defeated wince, and receives only a snort of contempt in return. She lashes out at the door control. Doesn't say a word.

I'm tentative, still unsure of the stability of this new power dynamic, but Pac is through the door before I even take a step. His hand trails through the frost, eyes wide with wonder. He pulls a sonic wrench from I don't know where and sets course for the closest connection, and I know that if it were up to him, he'd spend the rest of the mission pulling everything apart just to see if he can put it back together again.

Ester and I circle it slowly, trying to take it all in. I take a deep breath, step in, and brush ice away from one of the stubby, black tubes that hangs just below the dish. Up close they are as thick as my torso, almost as long, and studded with silver. I peer at the caps, at small etchings on the curved surface of each one. Indecipherable squiggles, sure, but they're too neatly formatted to be an accident.

"Ester, look at this. These are markings. I don't recognise them. Do you?"

I glance back in excitement, only to find revulsion written across Ester's features, and the studs, their markings, what they might mean, it all falls from my mind. I find myself studying her, our Matre, trying to imagine what it is she's looking for. What it is she sees.

Her hand unconsciously clasps the Ring of Eden she wears around her neck. Her lips curl back, baring her teeth. I turn from her to the object, and it hits me like a jolt from a shorted circuit.

She sees what I see. A sign from Eden.

But where I find hope, a spark, a link to our common past out here in the vast unknown, all she sees is danger. A reminder of how our ancestors went too far, and brought down the Retribution. She sees a warning: turn back, lest you make the same mistake.

She backs away, lips fluttering in a fervent, silent prayer. I want to follow her, to reassure her, to show her that what we've found is a part of our history, that by denying it we are cutting ourselves off from our future. But I don't.

It's too big a risk.

"Trill! Come look at this!" Pac yells from across the room, and the bright sound penetrates the brooding silence. I glance back at Ester, then at the door, and see Trill is still simmering just beyond it.

"Trill, come on! You've got to see this!" He waves madly at her, giddy with excitement, and the purity of it thaws even Trill's pride. Not much, her arms are still firmly crossed, her glare as deadly as the radiation that poisons every planet we've surveyed far, but enough. Enough to cross the threshold.

Pac meets her half way, one of the boxes partially dismantled in his hands. "This coil here. What does it remind you of?"

Trill peers down in that judgmental way of hers that says she's already decided he's wasting her time, all she's weighing is whether or not to berate him for it.

Then her eyes widen, and I swear I see the shockwave travel down her spine.

"Is that...?" She pokes a finger, then retracts it as if she's been burned.

"What else could it be?"

I've never seen such unconstrained wonder. Her attention moves from Pac's box to the other half-dozen or so widgets that cling to the same structure, and she studies them with a curious recognition. Discovery is in the air and I have to be part of it. The sense is so strong that it washes Ester's continuing revulsion completely away.

I race to be with them, my hand trailing along the folded edges of the machine's octagonal body, ice melting beneath my fingertips. They trace clean edges and rough, straight edges and round, and I'm beyond it before the strangeness of what I've just uncovered registers in my mind. A streak of brilliant gold amongst the dull metal, a roundel, standing proud beneath the ice. I swipe it clear and it hangs there like a light fitting retrofitted into an unexpectedly dark corridor. Shining. Covered in markings.

And not just markings.

Diagrams.

An explosion of lines from a central point. Concentric rings bounded by a pattern of vertical and horizontal marks. Wave-forms with dimension markers, stacked one atop the other. Rectangles. Circles–

Rings. Two of them. Connected by a line.

My breath catches. Tears blur my vision, and still I see it, as if the image had been imprinted on my mind: Rings of Eden. Not one but two.

Two rings. Two Eden's. The home we forgot, and the home to which this disc will guide our imminent return.

Hope solidifies into certainty.

None of this has been an accident.

We were meant to be find this, all of us.

"Quae? Are you alright?"

It's only with the intrusion of Pac's voice that I realise I am shaking, my body and my lungs betraying an absolute loss of control. All I can manage is to point.

Pac crouches slightly, bending to examine my discovery. He runs his fingers across it, feeling the ridges left by the etchings, leaving smudged fingerprints on its pristine surface. A puzzled blankness flashes across his features and he turns back to me with a shrug.

"What do you think it is?"

"I...." I want to tell him, but the words catch in my throat. I feel, or maybe I imagine, Ester's fear of the ungodly, her growing certainty of the blasphemy inherent in this machine. She cannot be allowed to know.

"Schematics of some kind?" Pac cocks his head to one side, tracing the wave patterns, glancing between them and the instruments he's in the middle of unpacking. "Trill, this is right up your–

"Quae." Ester's hand slips inside my elbow, and her fingers close tight around my forearm. Her voice is close, cloying, weighted with horrific calm. "I think it's time we began recalculating our route. Don't you?"

She knows. Bile rises in the back of my throat. *She knows because I told her.*

I wrench my gaze away from the golden circle, its incomprehensible etchings, the clues to our salvation I'm certain are hidden in the jumble. I wince as I look her way and... she's watching me. She's not looking at the golden circle at all.

She raises her eyebrows, widens her eyes, as if waiting for me to agree, to walk away from this incredible discovery just like that. Trill slides across, fasteners and lids, springs and brackets trailing in her wake, and Ester tugs at my arm, pulling me close.

"You feel it too, I know you do." She whispers in my ear. "We have to get them out of here, away from this thing."

Relief floods through me, so warm that it prickles my skin. I don't think that. At all. But she thinks I do, and that means she doesn't know. Not yet. And if I play my cards right, I can keep it that way.

I nod, feigning uncertainty, pleased at my sudden cunning.

"This is a test." She looks away, talking to herself now. She stares at the giant dish, at the three pronged temple rising from its depths. "I knew it as soon as I saw it, and what did I do?"

You did what I wanted, for once, I think. *Will you do it again?*

Trill drags Pac back to their dismantled gadgets, leaving the golden disc unattended and shimmering under a fresh layer of frost. This is my chance to pull them all away. Regain Ester's trust. Keep the disc of gold safe.

"We've forgotten the purpose of the rituals, Matre."

"Yes." Ester nods, running her fingers through her damp hair, her back straightening, her shoulders pulling back. With that one action, the Ester of old has returned. "Brother Pac!"

He raises his head from his jumble of components, but when he sees Ester's stance, the hardness of her features, the darkness of her gaze, his contented smile falls away. "Yes, Matre?"

"I need you to fetch my robes, and my calefactor."

"But Matre..."

"Pac, what does the Lord bid us to do with remnants of the fall?"

"I know, Matre, but..."

"Now, Brother." The cold command in Ester's voice is like a hand about my neck, and the way her authority weaves through him, the way he sags and slinks away without looking back twists my intestines into knots.

Trill half stands in protest. "Ester–

"You were right. I should never have allowed you in here with this... corruption."

"This *thing* is a satellite. A probe just like ours." Trill snaps, waving at the disordered mess of our probes, our instruments, tossed about by our emergency deceleration, and my mouth falls open as I see that she is right. "It's just old."

"If it is old, it is not like ours. Old is tainted. Old is unpure. Old brought us to the brink–

"And old saved us! Every ship in the fleet is ancient, and they keep us alive!"

"And every single ship, if left uncleansed, would have brought about our end just as they did for our ancestors. It was our piety, not your science, your striving for knowledge, that saved us. We survived through our purity of hearts." Ester snatches a connector out of Trill's hands. "Through our faith."

"Where was your faith when the *Refuge* was lost in the jump? When the *Strident* lost power, and fifteen thousand souls suffocated in the dark? What were your brother priests doing while our ships failed and our people died? I know what *I* was doing."

"I've suffered your arrogance, your blasphemy, time and again, because you've always been focused on the mission. But not this time." Ester steps forward, and Trill stumbles back, a dismantled lens skittering away where it jammed beneath her feet. "You say this thing is a satellite, just like ours, but it's not like ours. Our probes, which you designed, which I cleanse and purify before every launch, exist so that we can find our people a new home.

"This, however, is a distraction. This is dangerous. This is everything that our forebears turned their backs on to keep us safe, and yet here you are, tinkering while your precious mission languishes!"

Trill glances over at me, pleading for my help, but I can only stare at my shoes. Ester cares about the mission only insofar as its failure proves the purity of her faith. I know this, but can I prove it, without outing myself?

She reaches up, grabs Trill by her collar and forces her eyes to the empty racks where our final probes should be, at the delicate instruments scattered across the floor, tossed about by our deceleration, all of which need to be recalibrated before they'll be of any use.

"What's more important to you? Wasting time, or putting those back together so we can get on with our mission?"

Trill straightens, hardens where Pac had sagged, swells where Pac had withered, and I fear Trill once again sees my satellite just as Ester does. As a distraction. As a threat. Oh Eden, what have I done?

I stare longingly at the golden disc, at the promise it holds, mere metres away and suddenly untouchable. Forbidden, out of everyone's reach.

Including mine.

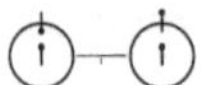

ESTER SHRUGS INTO HER robes, her calefactor glowing red hot, and locks herself into the launch bay. She forges wards and mutters prayers, not to purify the 'heretical relic', but to protect us from its stain. Just her and her certainty against the Retribution of her Lord.

When she's done she sends me away, back to the cockpit, leaving a shrunken Pac to right fallen probes and straighten damaged mechanisms under Trill's agitated shadow. I slide into my seat and stare at my nav console. I check and plot, re-focus, re-check, re-plot. Knowing exactly where I've gone wrong, wondering how I can possibly get back on track.

I had it in my hands. Eden. Real and tangible, just as my mother taught me, and the moment I'd felt threatened I had acted out of fear. For one glorious hour we had Ester on the back foot, and in my panic I'd allowed her to reassert control.

I shuffle over to Pac's chair and watch the distant stars spin by as our trajectory resets. I put us back on the path I'd calculated so long ago. A path to a planet that we all know offers no hope, no chance of salvation.

My jaw is clenched tight, so tight that it hurts. Trill is wrong. Her mission is a failure, only her obstinance won't let her see it. But the golden disc; I trace its etchings in my mind. The bursting lines, the strange diagrams, my finger skittering across the surface circling the twin rings. The twin Edens. Our once and future home.

That is where our hope lies.

I have to get it back.

I turn for the launch bay, and an otherworldly tension flickers behind my eyes. A familiar sensation, like my brain is half a step behind the rest of me.

The jump.

I swivel, and my mind sloshes, realisation slowly blooming. Ester has performed the ritual without me. I take a step but Trill is already in the cockpit door, leading Pac, leading Ester. Getting us back on track.

She glares at me, as if I'm an obstacle too. Ester looks through me, as if I'm not even there. Pac, for his part, doesn't look my way at all.

"Shipspirit, commence the cryo-sequence." Ester barks, all pretense at reverence gone. I stare wistfully down the corridor leading back to the launch bay, but there is no-one else. No way out.

Ester guides us into our cryo-pods and watches closely as the covers close, one by one. A smile curls across her lips and stays there, never reaching her eyes. I look away. Try to picture myself in my navigator's chair, just as I always do. It's better than lying here knowing I've been beaten. That I defeated myself.

A brand new planet will be right there, just beyond the viewscreen, its vast oceans and swaths of pristine cloud, just waiting to be explored. Chill curls my toes, and the image twists. I look down and the golden disc is in my lap, the blue and the white reflected on its surface.

I run my fingers across it once more, and this time, they don't skitter, they don't smudge. For a reason I can't discern, I move beyond my twin Edens, to the exploding lines by their side. Fourteen lines radiating outwards from a central point.

The cold runs up my chest and I can feel the blackness coming.

I fight it, holding on for dear life.

Fourteen lines. Not Spreading. Converging.

The mist surrounds me. There's no planet anymore. No nav chair. My legs, the disc, the console all fading away–

The console.

I force my eyes open, resisting the cryo-mist all the way. There is only white and cold and stillness but I dig my frozen nails into my numb thighs and that sharpness keeps me thinking, for just long enough.

Fourteen lines, fourteen symbols.

Fourteen points of reference.

A map.

The disc is a map, and at the centre is Eden.

Salvation.

Coated in gold.

My hand falls slack, the mist devours, and I sleep.

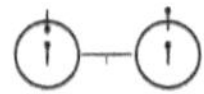

It feels like an age has passed, and also only an instant. I'm awake, and I have a plan. I hold that image of the golden disc in my mind and force myself to act as if I've forgotten. I don't look to Pac, I don't avoid Ester. We're all too tired, too woozy and we fall into our habits as if this was just another jump.

Trill heads unsteadily for the shower, Ester sure to be hot on her heels. Cryo-sleep always seems to hit her the hardest. Pac wipes himself down. He knows better than to get involved in that scramble. He knows me, too. Knows my ritual, and he eyes me warily as I slip away and into the corridor.

I can't afford to give Pac, or anyone, reason to follow, so I do what I've always done. Stumble down to the cockpit, collapse into my chair, marvel at the new planet, P0711M, floating in the distance.

It doesn't match my vision. There are no oceans, no clean white clouds. P0711M is just desert and rock, orange, brown and black, and all of it tinged with that tell-tale sickly green. Before I would have prayed, pushed beyond the evidence of my senses, offered this planet a name. But not today.

I stay in my seat for no more than two minutes. Just long enough for Ester to relax into her shower, the habitual self-cleansing that comes before all else for her. I pull myself shakily to my feet, cringing at every pop and creak of my joints. Only when I'm free, and sure that I'm alone, do I tiptoe back down the corridor.

I don't plan to stay in the launch bay for long; only to liberate the golden disc from its fixings. I snatch at Pac's ultrasonic fastener and duck beneath the dish, weaving between the sacrificial relics hung strategically by Ester as wards against some imagined corrupting force.

Blood rushes in my ears as I press up against the golden disc. My eye falls instantly to the bursting star and with a flush of pride, of excitement, I know I was right. It's a map. It can't be anything else.

I thumb the switch to 'undo', and listen for the telltale hum of fasteners loosening. I hold the disc tight against the panel with my free hand. A rattle of something falling, a soft beep, and I'm in. The ultrasonic fastener, job done, sits forgotten at the base of the dish, and with both hands I ease the disc away.

A scrape. A clunk.I freeze. Press my cheek up against the cold metal of the surrounding panel and listen. Hah! The disc is not just a disc. It's a container. There's something else inside.

Gently, slowly, I lower the cover, revealing another golden disc. This one is slim, the surface almost entirely covered in slender, concentric grooves. The centre is flat, etched with far more intricate, but still unfamiliar, markings, and I see that it wasn't this disc that was scraping and clunking. It sits anchored by a central pivot, fixed to the inside of the cover.

No, rattling around inside is a small, articulated arm pinned to one side of the outer shell. It's about the length of my hand and three times as thick, with hinges that creak in protest against any movement. I swivel it upwards, run my fingers along its length and–

"Aah!"

Pain, short and sharp. My finger flies to my mouth and I jerk, clamping both discs to my chest with my uninjured hand, lest they clatter to the floor. I taste salt and iron leaking from my fingertip.

Deep breaths, Quae, deep breaths. I inspect my finger. A tiny spec of red seeps along the ridges of my fingerprint. Nothing major, just a prick. I eye the innocent looking appendage with a hint of spite, wary of its pointed tip.

There are scratches on the outermost edges of the inner disc, where the pin has dug into the metal. I glare at it, as if it has damaged my prize on purpose. Why are you here? What are you for?

What are your makers trying to say?

A short burst of muffled anger echoes down the corridor, a timely reminder that I'm in forbidden territory, smuggling contraband. I flick the offending appendage back down, its vicious spine tucked safely away in the small gap between the inner disc and its casing and rise to my feet. I'm not built for stealth, but I make the best of what I have.

I tiptoe towards the mess hall. Have these corridors always been so long, so well lit? Angry words grow nearer as I creep, then clearer, and suddenly they're right on top of me. Pac bursts into view as I duck awkwardly into the med-lab. Our eyes meet, and for a split second I see him smile. There is a spark there, a defiance I thought lost. I know exactly where he's headed. I press my back against the bulkhead, grinning like an idiot, as first Pac, then Ester storm past.

I squeeze my eyes shut, try in vain to calm my breathing. I count ten heartbeats, and then ten more. Ester's shouts echo then shift, as she follows Pac from corridor to launch bay. Otherwise, all is silent. The inner disc's grooves are soothing against the palm of my hand. I steel myself. It's time to move.

I pass empty rooms to my left and right. No sign of Trill. My footsteps are like hammer blows to my ears and I am certain that at any moment Ester will hear them over the sound of her anger, that she'll come surging after me.

But she doesn't, and I'm back in the cockpit unscathed. I slump into my chair in the way only a euphoric fugitive can, and pull the inner disc free. I want to study them both. Uncover their secrets.

The polished gold gives the reflected light of P0711M an oily sheen. I gaze at that map for a long time, at the twin Eden's, desperate to know what they mean. I wish my mother could have been here. I wish I could show her what I've found.

"I've always loved that melody."

I didn't even realise I was singing. The Edensong's final bars catch in my throat, and my face scrunches as if in pain. Trill. I don't even bother to turn around. She slides deftly into Pac's chair and we're side by side

"I didn't know you knew it." I let my head fall back into the gap beneath my headrest.

She leans across, her elbow digging hard into the arm-rest. "Are you going to let me see?"

I eye her warily. Where has this come from? To her the disc is a distraction from the mission. Her mission. She's a chemist, a planetary biologist. She wants to know why so many planets have rejected us, and if they're recovering. She wants to unpick the patterns, one measurement at a time. The fallen structures, ruined cities, all the remnants we've uncovered of what came before, they've just been in the way. Until now.

"Why?" I hold it close, and something I can't unpack flashes across her features.

"Why? Because it's unique. Anyone with a brain can see that."

"It's not a distraction?" I feel like a petulant child.

"Not right now. Not for the next hour or two at least."

I purse my lips. I want to think of the disc as mine, but it's not. It's ours. All of ours. Trying to hold it back is what got me in this mess. Hesitatingly, I hand the outer casing over. "Careful. There's a spike on the back. It's sharp."

She takes it from me as if I haven't even spoken and stares at it intently. She flips it over, flips it back. Her lips move as her eyes trace the lines and markings.

"This is a map."

I shift in my seat, uncomfortable with Trill, the single minded scientist, suddenly devoting her attention to an article of my faith. "Yeah, I–"

"And an instruction manual. These markings." She traces the dashes that encircle the concentric rings. "Do you recognise them?"

"I was wondering if they might be binary notation..." My voice trails off, my gaze fixed on the pictogram embedded in the left hand side of the largest concentric circle. It's the arm, right down to the point. I pick up the inner disc, holding it by the edges. It has the same three rings: the outer ring where the arm was sitting and where the grooves start, the inner where the grooves end, and the hole in the centre.

"--re you listening, Quae?"

"Yes. I mean, of course." I mutter, unconvincing even to myself. If the vertical and horizontal dashes are binary notation, then the markings that ring the inner disc must be a number. But what number? The circumference? I flip the inner disc so that I'm looking at just the edge. There's another diagram showing the same view with another number, this time the radius–

"Then what did I just say?"

"Look, just give me a moment, alright?" I brandish the inner disc at her, displaying it right in her overly serious face. "This is the disc in the diagram. If we can just figure out what these numbers are–"

"Oh put that down. If you'd just listened instead of daydreaming..." She waves the disc away, and somehow she manages to make my excitement feel juvenile. She points at my Eden. At our salvation. "Look here. Does this mean anything to you?"

I can't speak. I can't even breathe. What can I possibly say–

"No, I thought not. This is more chemistry than star-mapping, but..." She glances up at me, her tongue playing across her lips. She's choosing her words, trying to make sure I understand. "I think this circle here is a hydrogen atom. I think they both are. This one on the left, it's electron has a positive spin, while the one on the right–"

"Is flipped." I nod, and something bright, something beautiful, something hopeful, begins to drain away. Not Eden, not Home. Hydrogen. So basic. So fundamental. And yet I had seen what I wanted to see. Was I so different, then, from Ester? But Trill doesn't care about any of that. The words fall from my lips, as if I'm reciting from an old nav manual. "Which means that the line connecting the two atoms–"

"Is the hydrogen line. It has to be." Trill's smile is as wide as mine should be, the dusty orange of the looming planet reflecting in the whites of her eyes. The hydrogen line. A physical constant, a measurement of both distance and time, one of the building blocks of the universe. A curiosity. A concept. But not a sign. Not salvation.

"And look here." She points to the small vertical dash beneath the line. "It's not connecting the two atoms, it's between them."

My heart beats so heavy in my chest that I feel nauseous. My head is spinning, pulled in totally opposite directions. Binary notation means numbers, and now we know what 'one' is. How long 'one' is. I stare at the diagram of the inner disc, and it seems to spin with me. I stare at the map, at the mystery slowly unravelling before me, at once gaining coherence and losing all meaning.

Trill is talking again, but I zone her out completely. My focus is all on me. Mindlessly, I twist the inner disc in my hands, P0711M's harsh reflection flashing across the grooves.

It takes a moment to register, but when it does my hands freeze, holding the disc up to the light. There, on the outer edge of the grooves, is an opening. They're not rings, closed off, forever separated from one another just as Ester preaches the Retribution separated us from Eden. That opening is the beginning, of one very long spiral.

Suddenly the diagrams, the articulated arm, the sharp pin make sense. Whoever made this is telling me how fast to spin the disc, how long it should take. I snatch the cover out of Trill's unsuspecting hands and flip it over on my lap. I slide the inner disc home over its pillar, slot the pin gently into the outermost groove. I work with a fervor born of my desperate need for meaning, spinning the inner disc about the central pillar, the pin scraping softly along the groove.

And that's it.

"Why did you do that?"

"I thought it would..." I trail off. What *did* I think would happen? That my spinning this flimsy circle would, somehow, resurrect the foolish hope I'd imagined this disc represented? That its makers might reach out and tell me what I, what we all, so desperately needed to know? Colour floods my cheeks, and I want to sink through the bottom of my chair, through the cockpit floor, and out into orbit. At least there I'll be alone, with no-one to intrude, to show just how childishly futile my dreams really are.

If Trill notices my turmoil, she gives no indication. Instead she them from my lap and, with fastidious care, holds them together and flips them over.

"Oh, well of course. I can see why you would." She mutters directly at the casing, at its diagrams and durations, as if it was the fellow human, and I the object of observation. She flips it back over, squints. "Mmmmm."

"What?" I can't help myself. What does she see that I can't? Jealousy prickles in my gut. If she wanted to uncover the murmurs of an ancient past then she should have sided with Pac and I, not Ester. The thought rings hollow in my head, adding a pang of guilt to my collection of regrets. I sided with Ester first. Not her.

"Brilliant." She pays me less than no attention. On the disc, her finger traces the long spiral, and on the cover she taps the etched diagram of the waveform. "Here. Hold this."

The whole contraption is pressed against my chest before I know what's happening. Trill is up, almost out the door. She catches the frame with her trailing hand, pulls herself back. "Figure out how fast you're meant to turn it. I'll be right back."

She's gone before words even begin to congeal in the slop that constitutes my mind. I stare after her, down the empty corridor, trying to parse all that just happened. The discs. Spinning the discs. Did she just say I was right? That I was brilliant? I feel dizzy, unable to handle such wild swings in my emotions.

I set the inner disc and the arm to one side, so I can focus on the cover. On the task I've been assigned. A wild idea forms. My hands tremble, and I speak to the stars. "Shipspirit, can you read binary notation?"

"YES, QUAE, I CAN READ BINARY NOTATION."

My eyes bulge. The shipspirit knows my name!

"Can you read this number here?" I hold the casing up to... I don't know where, and I trace the binary notation encircling the representation of the inner disc.

"5,113,380,864." The answer is instantaneous.

I close my eyes, unable to quite believe what is happening. "And can you tell me the period of the hydrogen line waveform?"

"7.040241837..."

I roll my eyes. "Five significant figures is plenty."

"$7.04242e^{-10}$ SECONDS."

Negative ten. That lines up perfectly. "Multiply those two numbers together." Sweat mingles with the cryo-residue on the hollows of my palms. "Please."

"3.6 SECONDS."

3.6 seconds.

I can't seem to get my breathing to stay in sync with my lungs. 3.6 seconds. It's such an ordinary sounding number. That can't be a coincidence. The hydrogen line, binary notation. Timings, not lengths. Trill was right. I trace my finger across that beautiful number one last time before flipping the casing over.

We were both right.

I'm just setting the pin in the starting groove when Trill bursts back into the cockpit. I glance up, and turn back again in surprise. I'd thought I was used to her chaos, but there is a manic gleam in her eyes, in the sheer width of her smile. She's panting, out of breath "Did you figure it o–"

"3.6 seconds."

"3.6? You're sure?"

I nod. "I'm sure."

"It's such an ordinary number!" She beams at me, brighter even than the ever growing planet just outside the window.

"I know, right?" I'm on my feet, holding the assembled discs out to her, doing my best to pretend that I can match her excitement, that I'm not teetering on the brink. My hands tremble. Trill takes them with one hand, squeezes them tight. In her spare hand she holds a dull grey dot, and a speaker.

She peels the backing off the dot with her fingernail, revealing a strong adhesive, and sticks it firmly to the head of the articulated arm. She presses the dot and the speaker, and the cockpit is filled with a low static hiss. I look around for somewhere to put the assembly down, somewhere level. Somewhere that won't rattle, won't create interference. In the end, I set it all down on the still warm seat of my chair. The playback clicks and clatters and finally settles.

Trill's eyes meet mine, and she bows just slightly.

I exhale slowly, lower my hand to the centre of the inner disc. I figure it will be easier to control the rotational speed from the middle.

I twist.

There's a clunk. A series of static clicks, and then a low hum, and I realise I have no point of reference, no internal clock. I watch the red clock on my nav console, trying to adjust my speed so that the disc's central pattern reverts itself in line with what I think is right.

And then it happens. Sounds. Irregular. Incomprehensible. I'm so focused on attaining the right rotation that I almost tune it out. But it sinks in regardless, because it's not just sounds. It's words.

Crackling, jumbled, running together as my fingers slip, but there's no mistaking it. Words. Sentences. A speech. Human speech. I feel light headed, as if I'm drunk, cryo-buzzed, as if I've just had sex and been for a run and laughed so hard I couldn't breathe. My hand falters, the disc scrapes and the words slow to a bass drawl.

"Keep going!" Trill urges, and I'm trying to find that sweet spot again, feeling for it with my gut. The words lurch and squeal and they're back, in all their unintelligible glory. I can't believe what I'm hearing, and at the same time I can. This is us, from so long ago, that every word has been forgotten. This is where we came from. And maybe, just maybe, this could be the start of our journey back.

I look up at Trill, wanting nothing more than to share my joy, and I freeze. My fingers go rigid and the voice screeches.

Ester.

She demand's silence.

The orange of P0711M's reflected light lends her body an ethereal glow, and she's standing back just far enough that her face is shrouded in shadow. The effect only serves to enhance the fury in her eyes. She's framed by the cockpit doorway but not bound by it. She has no robes, no grooming, no accoutrements of power, and still it could never contain her. Not like this. Trill's shudders back, the excitement of our discovery leaching out of her. She doesn't need to turn around. She can feel the chill in the air.

"Shipspirit. Halt recording and erase." Ester's voice is ice cold, the humanity stripped away. Its contrast with the fuzzy, almost gentle rambling of the words on the disc sends me right back to the seconds before cryo-sleep. To the fight to stay conscious. In control.

"DO YOU WISH ME TO MAINTAIN A BACK-UP, MA-TRE?"

"No. No back-up." Ester's eyes don't leave mine.

"RECORDING HALTED. RECORDING ERASED."

"Shipspirit, confirm launch bay is unoccupied."

"CONFIRMED, MATRE. NO LIFE SIGNS PRESENT IN THE LAUNCH BAY.

I should say something, but gravity, inertia, my own weakness, they all conspire to keep me silent. I just let her do it.

"Ester, wait–"

Ester cuts Trill's protest off with a look. "Shipspirit. Open the launch bay doors and evacuate all *non-mission critical* materials." Trill winces. Closes her eyes.

I feel the rumble of the doors through the ship's structure, the clang and scrape of our discovery, mine and Pac's, and now Trill's, slipping back into the emptiness. Into an unstable orbit around a dead planet, destined to burn to ash, its story lost forever. I hug the discs to my chest.

"Give them to me." Ester steps into the light, and she is a stranger to me. Almost alien. The woman who shared her doubts and her fears while kneeling on the floor, who hesitated and allowed us to explore an unknown thing, that woman is gone. Was gone the moment I encouraged this Ester to return.

The launch bay doors close with a thunk, and a horrid thought descends, taking root in my gut. "Where's Pac?"

"I hand them over, Quae. We go back to the mission and this goes no further."

"Ester?" Trills pulls herself upright, towers over her. "Where's Pac."

It's not a question.

"Pac re-affirmed his faith. You will too." For the first time, Ester's facade falters. Just for a moment. "That... that *thing* was a blasphemy. A temptation, sent by the Lord to draw us from our path. From our mission. You've been taken in by it–"

"Where is he?" I'm standing too, now. Two against one, if it comes to that.

"Do you even see yourself? You huddle here in secret, listening to a corruption long buried, letting it poison you. Poison those around you." Ester glares at Trill. "Those who had promised they were loyal."

I stare at Trill, but she avoids my gaze, and there is shame in her eyes.

"There is no corruption here." I protest. "Those voices are us! Only us! I know it!"

"*...and lo, we were the agents of our own destruction.*" Ester recites, pointing an accusatory finger at my chest, at the discs clutched tight in my arms. "You've never believed, I saw it from the start and yet I said nothing. I should never have allowed you to step foot on this ship. You're a danger to this mission. To the fleet. And so are they."

I back away, but there's nowhere to go. I press against the nav console with my thighs, my free hand scrabbling behind me for something to hold, a lever, a handle, anything.

"Why are you letting her do this?" I scream, and Trill looks away. "You heard it! You know!"

Ester is so placid, so terrifyingly calm. "Pac?"

"Yes, Matre?" Pac shambles into view, and the light I saw in the corridor only half an hour ago is gone from his eyes.

"Get them off her."

He stalks towards me, and I scramble up onto the console. My head hits glass, and it's cold and smooth against my the back of my neck. I bring my knees up to my chest and cradle the discs against my stomach. I try to remember the words that Ester wants me to forget, the soft timbre, the quiet command, the crackle of a recording millennia old. I try to remember my mother, singing the Edensong, holding me tight.

Nothing comes. All I can see is Trill, trying to melt into the shadows, and Pac, his features empty of emotion. His simple faith, twisted and contorted into violence. Behind it all I see Ester's manic certainty. Those sad, green eyes are all compassion, all pity, as if she truly wishes I could see what she sees but knows I never will. I know what she sees: a threat to everything she thought she knew, and she has imposed her fear on Pac. Forced him to act as her hands, even if it destroys him.

"Pac, what has she done to you?"

Ester answers for him. "I brought him back in from the edge."

He eases my knees apart, rests his hands on mine. Slowly, gently, he pries the discs from my fingers, and I let him. I tell myself it's because I can see how much this is hurting him. That if I fight he might break me, and that might break him. That I set all this in motion. That this is my fault, not his. That he shouldn't be the one who has to pay. Even if it means destroying our last hope of finding home.

But I know, deep down, that I let him because I'm weak. Because I don't know what else to do, how to stand strong against such fanatical conviction. My lip quivers, he pulls the disc free of my grip, and turns away without a word.

"What will you do with them?" Trill's voice is hollow, her body a shell.

"That is none of your concern." Pac hands the discs over, lays bare the completeness of our defeat. Ester glows. "Prepare the ship for an analysis run. We have a job to do."

I watch the glimmer of gold until the discs are out of sight. Trill stutters. She still won't look at me, but neither will she go. I've never seen her so uncertain.

I turn to face the looming planet, its curvature warped by the thick glass. I face away so she can leave, and I block all else out. There are only clouds, whorling in stasis, the last vestiges of P0711M's atmosphere clinging on, but also trapped and alone. Trill leaves without a word, and hot tears burn in the corners of my eyes.

I can only let them fall.

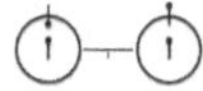

It's only at the shipspirit's implacable insistence that we all congregate in the launch bay to prepare our next set of probes for release. I sit mute at my station in the empty bay, mechanistically adjusting our trajectory and tracking what's left of my satellite as it slowly spirals into a doomed orbit, wondering which of the flickering specks on my nav screen is my golden disc?

I stare out at the planet through the open bay doors, wishing, but not expecting, to catch one last glimpse of the hope I let slip through my fingers. Soon they will hit P0711M's poisoned atmosphere and become just another meteor, burning away to nothing.

Ester stalks the sparse metal floor like the warden of her very own prison. Her glare passes through me as she shadows Pac. He sits with his back to me, setting and resetting the guidance system with a numb focus. I glance back at my screen, taking in nothing. I can't blame him for what he did. Only myself for giving in so meekly.

Trill is devoted to her instruments, while I fixate on the past. My stomach churns as a satellite fragment leaves streaks of superheated metal across the atmosphere, slashes of gold so brilliant against the charred earth below that I can't look away. The launch window almost passes by, completely forgotten.

Blaring red numbers, counting irrepressibly down, finally burn through the fog of my self-loathing. I start upright, weeks of routine driving me to open my mouth, to shout the one minute warning. Ester's eyes darken from behind Pac's shoulder. A look of pure triumph, and in that instant I know. That she's won, not just this battle but the war.

I see it as clear as if I had already lived it. She's bent us to her will. We'll complete the mission. This planet, the next and the next. We'll return to the fleet behind schedule, empty handed. The waiting crowds, our grandchildren, our great-grandchildren, they'll see it in our faces, and above the murmur of dashed hopes Ester will reluctantly, oh so reluctantly, fill the void.

She'll praise our efforts, lament our noble failure, and affirm that in fact, our mission was always doomed. That its conception was an understandable display of weakness from her forebears when confronted by the inevitability of our fate. That striving, even for survival, has always been our greatest vice.

She will look down upon the ecclesiastical council and, with a knowing finality, proclaim that the Lord's punishment has always been total. That our mission is living proof. That our path back to Eden can only ever be through humility. Through acceptance of the end we all know is coming.

Trill tightens the final fasteners, Pac bows his head in blessing and in thanks, and Ester's calefactor glows red hot. She fixes the ring to the probe's casing. Gives it her blessing, and the shipspirit carries it forth. The whole time, Ester's gaze never leaves mine. Not as she raises the empty calefactor to her forehead, not as she accepts Pac's offering, not even as she mutters the prayer of the fall and the rising.

The *Revenant* shudders from the launch, and only then does she allow me to look away, knowing that I know. Knowing that I let her, that I can only watch as the probe arcs down towards the same thin shell of radioactive air that is, at this very moment, devouring the last chance our people will ever have.

I should be angry. She knew what I'd found. Knew it would save us. Knew it would ruin her. I should be furious, yet all I am is empty. A vessel for converting nutrigel into course adjustments, oxygen into launch countdowns. The impact probe sets sail, the upper atmosphere spectrograph, the low altitude chromatograph. The bay, for now, is clear.

Trill slams her tools to the ground, glares at Ester and storms away. Even though I know she's only leaving to check the datastreams, that she'll be back to prep the final two probes no matter how much she might not want to, it's a show of defiance I can't even bring myself to contemplate.

Ester watches on with her back to me, a stray finger playing with her perfectly waved hair, and a thought penetrates the fog:

when does she find the time? We reach the nadir of our orbit, the guidance jets fire, and her hair, her robes of office gleam white against the blackness of space. I glance down at my stained underclothes, at my bare arms and legs and the flakes of cryo-slick peeling from my skin. There is no comparison between Ester and I. Absolutely none at all.

I stare at the cycling numbers, always counting down. At our projected path. The next launch is not for another 37 minutes, but there's nothing else for me to do. An entire world rotates away just out of sight, and I find myself praying. Not for Eden, not for my people, but for the merciful oblivion of cryosleep.

A shadow falls across my screen. My throat tightens, and for just a moment I luxuriate in the surge of emotion. It doesn't last.

"You know it had to be this way." Ester's voice is low, her tone magnanimous, her eyes anything but soothing. "Your yearning radiated like the sun, Quae. Like the abominations that sparked our downfall. If I had let it spread, it would have infected us all."

Ester forges on with her sermon, but I'm no longer listening. Trill's reappearance draws me in like a magnet. There's an energy about her; more than anger, more than defiance. She's framed by the doorway, a missile at the moment of launch, her target in her sights.

She catches me staring and my vision tilts, my empty stomach lurches. It's like I've been plucked from the depths of the cryo chamber mid-cycle. Sweat breaks out on my brow and my back-- and then Trill's vibrancy is gone, as if it never happened. She marches towards the empty probe that Pac has just dropped to the workbench, mute but for a single muttered sentence.

I'm listing sideways, peering around Ester, my gaze trained on the back of Trill's taut shoulders. Did I imagine it? I must have. Whatever I thought I saw in her eyes, in her manner, is gone.

There's only the three of us, sloughing our way through these next two launches with the minimum possible interaction. What is there to say? What can we say, with Ester right there watching?

And honestly, I prefer it this way. Each cross-check marked off the list, every time-call and every sentence kept bottled up inside is another moment I don't have to face it. Another moment I can block it all out and just do my job.

Call the launch, call the next. Close the door. Don't look back.

Focus on the trajectory, not the destination.

Don't think about what's been left behind.

Prepare the jump. Perform the ritual.

Ignore the bile rising in the back of my throat at the hollowness of Ester's prayers, the strains of doubt in Pac's face, that come only now that it's too late.

Feel the shudder and slip as we slide away between the gaps in reality, relieved that there's nothing left to do but sleep.

The cryo chamber beckons and I head straight for it. I don't even need to change. 43 hours and still I wear only my underclothes, dropping flakes of uncleaned residue with every stray brush of my arm. Already I'm visualising the coming nothingness, rushing through what must come before: a finger across the bioscanner, three lights flashing green. The snap-hiss of the cover as it opens and beckons, the cold sweetness of the ch–

"Isn't it amazing how, even today, she found the time to fix her hair?"

Trill's eyes blaze with a forbidden fire. She squeezes my trembling hand and she's away before I can blink. My jaw flaps in the still air and the fog.

I didn't imagine it! How could I? There's no mistaking the look in her eyes, the human embodiment of righteous retribution. I swivel, expecting to see Trill do what I could never, but again there's nothing. All that energy, gone. Ester is stepping out of her clothes and into her pod, Pac shadowing her every step, and Trill is exactly how she was before. Oozing her futile, directionless, impotent anger, flinging her jacket against the wall, her coveralls behind her. They hit me in the chest and fall against my feet.

My head is spinning. I can't parse what's just happened and all of a sudden I'm the last one standing. Ester and her perfectly coiffed fringe are all that remain visible of my crewmates. She looks upon me with pity.

"Come, Quae. Sleep will do you good, I'm sure of it."

I nod, hating that she's right. The chill, the cold, the dark. That's what I need. Not bizarre statements out of the black. I don't even glance Trill's way as I step, finally, into my pod. I lie back, running my fingers through my own ragged hair, and I freeze.

Four pod doors hiss in unison as they begin their descent, but it's not the cryo chill that's struck me dumb. She *didn't* have time! Of course she didn't! It was one or the other, not both, and she chose her hair, even now. Her grooming. Her outward facsimile of perfection.

The walls close in and I curse Trill with every piece of foul language I know. Why did she have to be so striving cryptic? If I hadn't been so wrapped up in my own self-pity, I might have seen it on my own. I might have understood what Trill was trying to say, instead of silently wishing she would enact my own desperate desire for reprisal.

The canopy is in the groove, sliding home, and my anger, my self-centred foolishness reflects back at me. But it's not too late. Not this time. My foot darts through the shrinking gap. I pray to the shipspirit, clamp my eyes shut and hold it there, not knowing what might happen.

"OBSTRUCTION. CYRO-SEQUENCE ABORTED. ADVISE CLEAR AND RESET."

The pod door recedes, the mist dissipates. I can't believe what I've just done. I glance down, and I can't keep the smile from spreading across my face.

Beside my foot, jammed in the mechanism, are coveralls.

Trill's coveralls.

"Trill! I could kiss you!"

My words echo in the empty chamber, easily dominating the slow burble of the crystal blue cryo-mist rising up my crewmate's legs. I take a tentative step out into the open. Trill has her fist clenched tight, pressed against her heart, Pac's wide lips have broken into a grin.

And Ester.

Her hands are pressed against the glass, her mouth open in a scream I cannot hear. I'm giddy with excitement, and I trail a finger through my knotted hair.

"I know you had to choose, Ester. Keeping up appearances is so vitally important." I feel cruel, gloating in this way when she's powerless to resist. The mist reaches her neck and yet still she fights it.

I glide across to her locker, watch her eyes bulge as I flick it open, drop her vestments to the floor. I could step on them, crush them beneath my feet, but I don't have it in me. Not when I see the glint of gold hiding in the back.

She slumps back, defeated. Cryosleep takes her. I mouth a prayer of thanks, for her vanity, for her pride, and for Trill, for seeing through the facade.

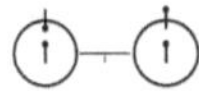

I TOY WITH SETTING my resurrected discs aside and allowing myself a shower, but I can't. I just can't. The discs' resurrection is a sign I cannot ignore, even for a moment. I make straight for Pac's workshop, and I barely make it through the door.

There, on the benchtop. A single word scrawled in the dust.

Sorry.

"Pac", I breathe, "I'm the one who should be sorry." I cast back across these last hours, from Trill blazing into the launch bay through to Pac shadowing Ester into her cryo-pod, and I realise that he hardly left her side, even for a moment. And still he managed to...

Hot prickles sting the corners of my eyes, but I fight them off. Now is not the time.

Beside his scrawl Pac has piled a hasty collection of gadgets, a mixture of forbidden and ancient. Motors. Crystals. Gears. Quantum Spirals. Even actual, physical wires. Everything I might need and more.

Three point six seconds per revolution. How hard can it be?

I set the discs down and get to work.

"Shipspirit, prepare to receive signal from vibration sensor C137."

"RECEIVING SIGNAL STRENGTH FIVE."

My heart beats loud in my chest, and not just because I am speaking with the shipspirit as if they are a collaborator. A partner in crime. I wonder if I'll be able to hear its voice over the rush of my own excitement.

"Record and playback output, please."

"RECORDING. PLAYBACK COMMENCED."

A single, deep breath. I press the switch.

And there it is. That voice. Those words. Different from how I remember, now that I can listen without fear of interruption. But still unmistakably human. They undulate, indecipherable, but clearly carrying a coherent message. I'm smiling so wide that it hurts.

And then it all changes. A different voice. Then another. And another. It seems that the words change too but I can't be sure. Ten seconds, maybe fifteen for each one, but no more. So many I lose count. Every now and then my pulse races as I think I catch half a word, a greeting maybe, but there's no going back, the voice gone until I return to the start.

They change again. Sounds now. Sounds I half recognise. Sounds from before the fall. Sounds from our life before we became trapped in the space between the stars. From when there were winds and storms, animals and trees. The sounds of a place we might have once called home.

A place we will call home again one day, if I can decipher this map.

I reach for the cover, trace my fingers across its lines. An animal howl falls away, replaced by the buzz of machinery. It's ancient, yes, but metal against metal sounds the same no matter when.

Each of the map's fourteen bursting lines has a number, in binary notation. A baby cries out, and it's as if a tiny hand has reached out of our past and is clutching the end of my finger. Trembling, I flick the switch. I need to think. The cry slows to a bass rumble and the disc slows to a stop.

"Shipspirit, can you convert these fourteen numbers for me? And multiply by the frequency of the hydrogen line for me when you do?" I add. No sense wasting time.

The shipspirit rattles off each of the fourteen numbers. All except the eighth are slightly less than one. But one what? If the numbers are anything like the numbers relating to the record, then it should be seconds, but this is a map. An astronomical map, and nothing in astronomy is measured in seconds. Except...

"Can you convert these fourteen numbers to cycles per second and compare against the frequency of known pulsars?"

The shipspirit is silent for a long moment. I can't breathe. What if I'm wrong? What if I'm right? My jangling nerves flick the switch and the baby's cry warbles one more time before it too fades away, to be replaced by an otherworldly pulsing, an ethereal scraping.

"NINE MATCHES AT 95% CONFIDENCE."

"Nine? Are you sure?" Nine! I'm on my feet, pacing. The surging hiss lurches into a series of warbles and trills. Nine! I'm so agitated it takes a moment for the auditory change to register as music. Spritely. Alive.

"I AM SURE, QUAE."

Too much is happening. Nine pulsars! The shipspirit! And music! My mind whirs. If each point is a pulsar, then the lines must represent relative distances–

The music changes, deep tolling bells replacing the soft, lifting melody. I stare at the record, marvelling at the sheer optimism of the creators of this disc, sending the words and sounds and songs of their people out into space in the hope that one day someone might find it and listen to it.

And it had come so close to destruction.

I'm shaking all over. I pace the room, hands on my head. I can't think. I have to force myself to breathe. The music changes again. Low, rumbling, with sharp clicks that accompany a droning chant, and it touches me somewhere deep.

Breathe, Quae.

Focus on the pulsars.

"Map those 9 pulsar's onto my nav console, and output playback via the cockpit speakers." I grab the cover, take one last look at the slowly revolving disc, and run.

The music follows me, changing again: up tempo, jostling vibrations, like a finger tapping against glass. It spurs me onward.

The cockpit is awash with the unnatural gleam of the jump, soft purples and uncanny yellows wash over me and the slippery tendrils of bare reality tickle my skin. The music changes: clanging riffs, driving beats, and the jump changes with it, shifting and jangling in time with the heart-tugging life of lyrics that I wish I understood.

My body wants to move with it, the urge is almost irresistible. Only the pulsing red of my nine reference points superimposed on our vast galaxy holds me still.

I set the cover beside the holomap and place my hand in the centre of the field. Now if I can just find the intersections of these lines...

A new song and my heart sinks. Haunting wails accompany an unwanted realisation. I have no reference for length, no reference for direction. All I have is nine points on a 3D map. I sink back into my chair and let the sorrowful music wash over me.

Slowly, I smile. All is not lost. It has been forty minutes since the disc started playing, and already I have nine reference points. I have seven months years before we reach our next destination. I can figure this out. I pick up the cover once more, let my fingers play across the surface.

The lines have angles. The lines have lengths. The music shifts again, a complex geometrical melody, rising and falling. My pulse quickens. There's a fifteenth line with no period, shooting off to one side. I glance at the cluster of pulsars, all of them collected in a single quadrant of our galaxy, and back to the solitary line, stretching away, far longer than the rest.

I click my fingers. I have it! The long line is the distance from the centre of the galaxy, and with that I have a reference distance. Reference angles, everything I need. A woman's voice breaks through like an angel, and at my command a red line feeds out from the first of the pulsars, then a second.

They don't intersect, but no matter. I have all the time in the world. Not even another collision will stop me now–

"Shipspirit! Plot the location of our intercept of the unknown spacecraft!" A green dot appears, right in the middle of the cluster of pulsars. Blaring, offbeat warbling accompanies my ragged breaths. "Now zoom in, plot its known trajectory and map against projected pulsar inclinations..."

The jump shifts once more, rivers of magenta and cerulean whorls rippling all around me. The stars rush away as my holomap zooms inwards, the trajectory of the lonely little spacecraft projecting back in time, chased by pulsing red, all of it converging on a single point–

The music shifts. Time stops, flies backwards, happens all at once.

I'm snug in my mother's arms, just the two of us alone, her voice resonating through me as she sings the forbidden refrains of Eden's lament.

And I'm right here, right now, alone in my navigator's chair, cheeks wet and chest heaving, as the first song my mother sung for me crackles from our speakers in a forgotten language, recorded on a disc of gold that we stumbled upon in the gaps between the stars.

And I know that one day, one day soon, I'll be at the head of the fleet. Pac flying, Trill planning, and me navigating.

Leading our people home.

AFTERWORD

I had the very first glimmer of an idea for this story back in 2022 after catching half of a feature on the radio about the Voyager spacecraft. It got me wondering about the Golden Records and what it would be like to stumble across them one day in the far future. And what if it was so far in the future that we'd forgotten we ever sent them out in the first place?

The Golden Record, both deciphering it and then experiencing its contents, play a critical part in *Homecoming*'s second act, and if you're not that familiar with Voyager or the Record I imagine that second act might get quite confusing. If that happened for you, my apologies.

To make up for it, I thought I'd compile some of the material I used to research this story, so you can get a feel for what was in my head as I was writing it (Quae's finale was written late at night, all in one sitting, synchronised with the audio of the Golden Record in my ears. That section of the story barely needed editing. It just flowed from my fingers) and maybe enjoy the story even more a second time around.

If you're interested in the Golden Record, what's on the cover, what's encoded on the record itself and how to read it, the best place to look is NASAs Voyager Hub (this link, and all the others, are on the next page). You'll find photos of the cover, the apparatus, all of the photos that were included on the record itself (crazy, right? I had no idea!), almost everything you could want.

If you want to listen to the golden record, then the whole recording can be found on youtube right here.

If you're a dork like me, and wanted to know exactly how to decode it, these are a couple of the resources I found, which I used to flesh out Trill and Quae's surreptitious investigations:

- Boing Boing: How I Decoded the Golden Record

- The Verge: Decoding Images from the Golden Record

And finally, just for fun, an Interactive 3D model of the Voyager Spacecraft (scroll down to the bottom of the page).

I hope you enjoyed the story, and thanks for reading!

Voyager & Golden Record Overview

Overview and Images

Listen

How to Decode the Golden Record

Boing Boing Article

Verge Article

Voyager Satellite 3D Model

ABOUT THE AUTHOR

Thomas is an Australian engineer, writer, and reader with too many books on the shelf waiting to be read and too many ideas scribbled illegibly in notebooks waiting to be written. When he's not staying up too late (sometimes writing, more often pro-crastinating) he can be found eating vegemite toast, watching old sci-fi shows, or getting far too invested in the footy (that's Australian rules football for the internationals).

Thomas lives in Melbourne with his partner and their dog. He writes (almost) every day flitting between crowd sourced flash fiction experiments, science fiction short stories, strange, unsellable novellas, thriller-leaning novels and the occasional un-finished, untitled fantasy epic. Most of which can be found on his website: thomaskslee.com

Thank you for reading *Homecoming*

I hope you enjoyed reading it as much as I loved writing it. If you think others will enjoy *Homecoming* too, then please consider leaving a review. Reviews help show readers that picking up a copy of *Homecoming* is worth their valuable time. They make a bigger difference than you may realise.

Review Now at
Goodreads

Get In Touch

If you have a question, want to suggest a topic or character for my next flash fiction adventure, or just want to say hello, then this is the place to go. You can send me a message direct, or sign-up for my monthly newsletter. I'd love to hear from you!

Get In Touch